T0188612

The perfect house, near the right
school, and thrillingly affordable.
How could Eleanor resist? A twenty-
something single mother, sharing
a room with her four-year-old in her
parents' house, she's desperate for a
new plan. This little bungalow, with
its yard and tree, feels like a lucky
gift.

It is only after the house is hers—
having eaten her savings and set to

devour her future income—that she realizes that something is terribly wrong. Investigating, she discovers her new neighbors: two ancient sisters who are feeding and fostering thousands of beloved "pets." And what had looked like a fairy tale turns out to be closer to a nightmare.

In *Devotion: A Rat Story*, Maile Meloy takes on the hopes and horrors of domestic life with a story that is riveting and exquisitely unsettling.

"She's such a talented and unpredictable writer that I'm officially joining her fan club; whatever she writes next, I'll gladly read it."
—Curtis Sittenfeld,
The New York Times Book Review

"Maile Meloy combines the meticulous realism of domestic fiction with the witchery of a natural-born storyteller."
—Laura Miller,
The New York Times Magazine

"Maile Meloy is a bit of a magician."
—Cleveland *Plain Dealer*

"In a Maile Meloy story, the thrill is in our own perception . . . [Her] style is disciplined and sly. She keeps a perfect poker face. And we're players in the game."

—*The Dallas Morning News*

"Don't let the easy accessibility of Maile Meloy's writing fool you; she's capable of witchcraft."

—*Time*

devotion

a rat story

devotion

a rat story

MAILE MELOY

RIVERHEAD BOOKS · *a member of penguin group (usa)* · *new york* · *2015*

RIVERHEAD BOOKS
Published by the Penguin Group
Penguin Group (USA) LLC
375 Hudson Street
New York, New York 10014

USA * Canada * UK * Ireland * Australia
New Zealand * India * South Africa * China
penguin.com
A Penguin Random House Company
Copyright © 2013 Maile Meloy
First published by Byliner, Inc., 2013
First Riverhead edition: 2015

ISBN 978-1-59463-459-8
Printed in China
1 3 5 7 9 10 8 6 4 2

Book design by Claire Naylon Vaccaro

devotion

a rat story

That the yellow house was thrillingly affordable might have been a warning sign, if Eleanor had known how to read it. But she'd been desperate. She was sharing a room with her four-year-old daughter, Hattie, in her parents' house, and she had to get out. Her parents didn't want her to leave, but that was part of the problem. What her mother really wanted was to have Eleanor back inside her, along with Hattie, nested like matryoshka dolls.

So when the neat bungalow came on the market, close to the school her daughter loved, Eleanor thought she'd made it up. A wish on a candle. The seller was a pixie-like blond songwriter who was never there and was selling it as is—another red flag. But Eleanor had never bought a house before, and the real estate broker had the air of an authoritative and impatient aunt, waiting for a decision. She tapped long nails on the steering wheel of her parked Lexus while Eleanor gazed at the little house from the passenger seat. The sycamore in the yard had good roots, the broker said.

"Won't someone outbid me?" Eleanor asked her.

"It's too small for most people.

And the seller thinks you're sweet. I think we can wrap this up, if we do it now." The broker tapped the steering wheel.

"You really think so?" Eleanor asked.

"Look, do you want it or not? You're getting manna from heaven, in your price range. What do you want, a burger?"

What Eleanor wanted was to ask her father to come walk through the house. But the broker already didn't take her seriously because she had a streak of pink in her hair and a bracelet of vines inked around her wrist. She didn't want to be the hapless tattooed girl who had to call her dad.

"No, I want the house," Eleanor said. "I do."

"All right, then," the broker said, dialing her phone.

The offer was accepted, and Eleanor promised her soul and her future income to the bank. It was a little dizzying. Her father raised his eyebrows at dinner. "Want me to look at it?" he asked.

"When I've got it all set up," she said.

"You've got an inspector?" her mother asked.

"The broker does."

"I want to see the house," Hattie said. She'd been refusing to use the booster seat because she was not a baby, and her head barely cleared the table.

"You will," Eleanor said. "You'll have your own room there."

Her daughter eyed her. Eleanor knew Hattie was thinking that she didn't really want her own room, but she wasn't going to be caught saying it.

"How about a real estate lawyer?" her father asked.

"It's a very straightforward transaction," Eleanor said.

At that, her parents fell silent. It
was fraught territory. They'd wanted
her to get a lawyer when Hattie was
born, too, but she'd refused. She had
met, in her last year of art school, a
boy as fierce in his independence
as she was, and their friends had
bet against the romance lasting six
months. When she got pregnant—
a broken condom—she discovered

that she had complicated feelings about fate, about why the latex had broken, about that particular sperm and that particular egg. James had moved to Australia. Struggling for his art wasn't going to include taking care of a baby. He had no money, and sending lawyers after him would only have prolonged the pain.

The first year was a blur of tears and lost sleep, a demoralizing return home, and her mother's delight in coming to the rescue. People felt sorry for Eleanor and sent her design jobs, and she took anything that was offered, staying up late after Hattie went to bed. Gradually the jobs turned into steady freelance work. She had saved money, living with her parents for four long years, and she had inherited a little more from her grandfather, and now she was trying to regain her own ground.

IT REALLY WAS a straightforward transaction. Escrow closed quickly, and she took possession right away. She bought two beds—an optimistically big one and a small one—and the mattress company delivered. There were no bookshelves in the house, but her father would help her build some. She drove her few boxes there by herself and was happy to be un-packing, making the beds, imag-ining her new life. Hattie would play in this yard and learn to climb the sycamore. Eleanor would get a swing set for the yard and hide Easter eggs in the spring, like her parents had done for her. She might even meet someone now, if she wasn't living at home.

She was bringing in another box,

thinking about what that someone might be like, when she saw an
enormous rat staring at her from the
front lawn. It gazed at her as if she
were the intruder.

"No," she said. But still the rat
stared.

She took a threatening step forward, and it darted away.

She carried the box up the walk,
haunted by the appraising way the
rat had looked at her, and saw another toast-colored blur disappear

along the side of the house. She called her father at work.

"There are rats here," she said.

"There are rats everywhere," her father said. "They live in the ivy."

"No, these are serious," Eleanor said. "They're *huge*."

"How huge?"

"Like small Chihuahuas."

"Oh." There was a pause. "Where are they?"

"One was on the lawn, and one running along the foundation."

"Should I come over?"

"Not yet," she said. "I don't want you to see it like this." She heard a small, patient sigh.

"Then call an exterminator," he said. "And stay with us tonight."

"I can't do that. It's admitting defeat."

"Defeat to whom?" he asked. "To your mother? Don't be a hero, Ellie."

"Do rats carry disease?" she asked.

"I think what they carry is fleas, and fleas carry disease."

"Oh, God," she said.

"Ellie," he said. "Call a professional and come home."

She hung up and searched for exterminators on her phone, and called one who could come the next morning. She tried not to think about how thrilled her mother would be to have her back.

Outside the school, she watched the other mothers: the tall, thin, grown-up, married mothers, with the diamonds on their fingers and the tiny pleated workout skirts. One wore a pink silk shirt printed with riding tack, without irony. They didn't have rats at home. Or fleas.

That night, her mother beamed with triumph over take-out pizza at the kitchen table. She said, "You know you can stay here as long as you like."

"It will be good to have our own place," Eleanor said.

"I don't see why," her mother said. "If it's I-N-F-E-S-T-E-D."

"What does that spell?" Hattie asked. She was already starting to read.

"She means the house is an invest-ment," Eleanor said. "A good thing to spend money on."

Hattie pushed a crust across her plate. *"Infestment,"* she said.

"If I'd known you were coming home," her mother said, "I could've cooked something special."

"It's not a special occasion, Mom. It's a temporary setback."

"It's *always* a special occasion," her mother said, tweaking Hattie's nose.

IN THE MORNING, in Eleanor's childhood bedroom, a battle raged. Hattie had two shirts that she was willing to wear, one red and one green. The green one was in a box at the new house. The red one was crusted with food and dirt from the day before. Hattie needed the shirts

in order to be Manuel, a boy she wor-
shipped at school. She didn't want to
be *like* Manuel, or even to be *liked* by
Manuel. She wanted to *be* Manuel.

It was understandable. Manuel
was handsome and dark-eyed, quiet
and popular and effortlessly confi-
dent. He was a natural athlete. When
they played catch, some of the boys
adopted a showy flourish of elbow
and knee, to make sure everyone was
watching. With Manuel, you barely

noticed the ball leave his hand. He was an efficient creature, with no wasted movement, and no apparent care for how he was seen.

Eleanor thought of her gay art history professor joking, "Whom the gods would destroy, they first make *women*." She wondered sometimes if Hattie identified as a boy. But she thought Hattie just wanted to be Manuel, and Manuel wore T-shirts in solid colors—like the green one

Eleanor had left at the new house, and the red one she had forgotten to wash.

"I don't want that one!" Hattie cried, pushing away a blue-striped shirt with a sailboat on the front.

"Hattie, please. We'll be late for school."

"No!" Hattie cried, throwing the striped shirt to the ground. Eleanor picked it up and tried to wrestle it over Hattie's head, but her daughter was surprisingly strong, and squirmed and fought free. She threw her naked torso onto the bed and sobbed heartrendingly into the quilt, her tiny vertebrae countable down into her jeans.

Eleanor wanted to cry with her. But she was the mother now, which was confusing. She had so recently been the daughter, allowed to fling herself facedown and weep. She wanted to ask if this was how Manuel would behave—cool, collected, unflappable Manuel—but she would only sound peevish and ineffectual. She had new compassion for her mother, especially when they weren't in the same room together. You just couldn't win, as a mom. She went to brush her teeth and let Hattie cry it out.

In the mirror, there were shadows like thumbprints beneath her aching eyes. The rats had invaded

her dreams: the ghostly touch of fur
against her cheek.

Back in the bedroom, Hattie had
taken the dirty red shirt from the
hamper and put it on. She turned,
wet-eyed and solemn, quietly trium-
phant in her red shirt.

"I am Manuel," she said. "Why is
Hattie crying?"

"I don't know," Eleanor said. "I
guess because she was sad."

It was always unsettling, this

transformation into the idealized boy in the correctly colored shirt, but Eleanor would take it if it got them out the door. She had known that she and James might produce a strong-willed and visual child, but she hadn't expected this obsession with color and identity, or the struggle that would be daily life.

In the chaos of the school drop-off, Eleanor caught sight of the real Manuel, standing by the steps. He was wearing a blue shirt. No stripes, no sailboat, but blue! Hattie didn't seem to notice. She didn't need to talk to Manuel because she *was* him now, calm and sure. She looked an inch taller as she carried her pink backpack inside.

Eleanor drove to her new street and parked to study the neighborhood. The yellow bungalow was there, still neat and unassuming on the east side of the street, dwarfed by the huge sycamore. The neighboring house to the south was a newly built stucco number with a clay tile roof. The builder had used every possible square foot, as usual, and the house was boxy and top-heavy, crowding the lot.

On the north side, beyond the sycamore and a wooden fence, was a two-story blue clapboard house, with a peaked roof and peeling paint. The picture window had heavy gray curtains hanging closed against the sunny fall day. The broker had warned Eleanor that two ancient sisters lived there, and when they died, it would be a teardown. In full rationalizing mode, Eleanor had decided that the tall fence would block the noise and the dust.

It was easy to choose which house to approach, when one looked like a witches' den and the other like a Taco Bell. She rang the doorbell of the boxy new house and heard the chime echo inside. After a minute a woman answered, in yoga pants and no makeup, her hair in a short silvery bob.

"I'm so sorry to bother you," Eleanor said. "This is an awkward question, but I just bought the house next door, and I was wondering if you've had any trouble with rats."

"I just came by to water the plants," the woman said, blinking. "The owners are away."

"Oh, okay," Eleanor said. "So—you haven't seen any rats?"

"Well, not lately."

"Lately?"

"I'm sort of not supposed to talk about it," the woman said.

Eleanor stared at her. "*Please* do."

"It's about property values, I think," the woman said nervously. "It really stresses them out, the whole thing."

Eleanor's stomach seemed to flip

over, like a pancake. "What whole thing?"

"You seem like a nice kid," the woman said. "Look, I didn't tell you this, but I think those ladies—the sisters—were feeding the rats." She started to draw back into the house.

"Wait!" Eleanor said, putting a hand out. "Please!"

"I have to go," the woman said, and she closed the door against the pressure of Eleanor's hand.

Eleanor stood a moment, listening to the soft footsteps draw away inside the house. Then she went to the yellow bungalow and walked along the high fence she'd thought would protect her from construction when the sisters were gone. The slats were too close together to see anything between them. So she went to the sycamore and got a handhold and then a foothold. The bark was pale and mottled, resilient beneath her fingers, and she climbed until she could sit in the yoke of the tree, holding on to a branch. She looked down into the sisters' backyard, where the grass was dead and the patio cluttered with broken furniture and cardboard boxes. Why had she never looked back here before? There were three shallow bowls set out, empty. There was a bag of cat food against the house. But she saw no cats.

Movement caught her eye in the

shadows, beneath a spiky, untended plant near the foundation. It took a moment before she could identify individual bodies. They seemed to cluster and confer, and then break up and gather again, on some urgent, mystifying business. They had matted gray fur and tails as big around as her finger. She tried to count them, but there were too many and they moved too quickly, disappearing into the darkness of the undergrowth and then weaving out again.

There was a basement vent without a cover, and they darted in and out of the dark.

Something moved in the tree and Eleanor flinched, but it was only the wind in the leaves. The sky was blue and cloudless between the branches. She climbed unsteadily down to the ground and stumbled away, feeling an enormous head rush, the world going briefly white.

"I KNEW THIS ADDRESS when you called," the exterminator said. He was bearish and bearded, in jeans. "I thought, Oh boy. She sold it, huh? The musician girl?"

Eleanor pressed her hands together to keep them from shaking. "She should be an actress," she said. "She gave a brilliant performance of someone with nothing to hide."

"She's nice enough," the exterminator said. "She was pretty frantic."

"Those women are feeding them *cat* food!" Eleanor said. "Why didn't she *disclose* it?"

But they both knew the answer. The musician girl had wanted out. The exterminator looked sympathetic.

"Didn't she call the health department?" Eleanor asked.

"Sure," he said. "But the sisters won't let the inspectors in."

"They *have* to," she said. "I'll call. I'll keep calling."

The exterminator nodded sadly, as if he had seen all this before: the hope of the new people who move into the haunted house, their determination to deal with the intransigent ghosts. "This has been going on for years," he said. "We're talking thousands of rats going in and out of there."

Her legs felt weak. "Oh, God, not really."

"Females mature in two months," he said. "They have five litters a year, if the conditions are good. Maybe eight in a litter? Half of those are females—I just want you to know what you're up against."

Eleanor didn't trust herself to speak.

"So maybe tens of thousands," he said, on reflection.

She nodded.

While he went outside to look for holes in her exterior walls, Eleanor drifted through the small, pretty rooms of the house. Everything she had was tied up in it: her income, her grandfather's money, her child's safety, her pride. When she got to Hattie's room, a rat sat up on its haunches on the crisp new sheets, inquisitive nose testing the air.

Eleanor turned and went out the front door and down the sidewalk. She walked around the fence, climbed the sisters' steps, and knocked. Her heart was pounding in her ears. She knocked harder, and something moved in the big curtained front window. Eleanor shivered but rapped on the door again, and would rap all day.

Finally it opened. The face that appeared in the crack had drooping, crosshatched skin and pale blue eyes, cloudy with cataracts. "What is it?" the woman snapped. She was so bent over she had to crane her neck to look up.

A frightening smell drifted out of the house, and Eleanor tried not to wince. Her throat was dry with fear. She felt like a neighborhood brat ringing doorbells. "I'm Eleanor," she said. "I just moved in next door.

I have a small child. I wanted to tell you that—our house is dangerously infested with rats."

The woman's milky eyes seemed to brighten.

"I understand that you feed them," Eleanor said. "I'm asking you not to. They carry disease. The exterminator is here, and I'd be happy to pay for him to—"

"Stop!" the woman cried. "How dare you come here?"

"I'm—your neighbor," Eleanor said.

"How dare you speak to me of ex-terminators?" the woman cried. "The rats have an unfeigned devo-tion that you will *never know*." She slammed the door.

Eleanor stared at the peeling paint, then made her way dizzily down the steps. There was no hand-rail. She was pretty sure that was not to code.

Inside the bungalow, the bearded exterminator was setting traps. She could feel the adrenaline in her body draining away. His concerned face wasn't reassuring.

"I don't see any new holes," he said. "The steel mesh I put in before is still in place. I think it's just the doors being open, while you're moving, that's bringing them in. They're curious. But don't poison them, whatever you do. It makes them die in the walls and then they stink."

Eleanor nodded.

"You okay?" he asked.

She shook her head and felt weak. "That woman next door said the rats had an unfeigned devotion that I would never know."

"Yeah, I don't think you'll get far with her," he said. "Escrow's closed and everything?"

She nodded.

"Call if you find anything in the traps. I'll come back and check to-morrow. You sure you're okay?"

She nodded again.

He put a strong hand on her shoulder, which under any other circumstance would have seemed wildly inappropriate, but she was grateful. When had anyone besides her parents last touched her in a reassuring way? Possibly the obstetrician, a round and cheerful mother of two, which didn't count.

She called the health department and was passed from one computerized menu to the next until it was time for the school pickup. When Hattie came running down the steps, in her dirty red shirt with her pink backpack, Eleanor's heart felt so full it seemed ready to spill.

She buckled Hattie in and drove home to her parents. She had been in such a rush to get away from her mother that she had bought a house full of vermin. Where had her caution been? Her due diligence? She was responsible for her daughter, for her safety. And really, her mother was a perfectly nice person. Well-meaning and popular among her friends. A leader in her book club, an excellent cook. An hour or two with her just drove Eleanor into a fetal position, rocking on her bed.

If she had been acting rationally, she would have brought her father to walk the property with her. She couldn't understand why she hadn't

seen the signs, and why the inspector hadn't seen them. She should
have found her own inspector. The
broker had an interest in selling the
house. Eleanor should have talked
to a lawyer like her parents had suggested. She should have looked in
the sisters' backyard. Her face felt
hot with shame.

"When do we go to the new house?"
Hattie asked from her car seat.

Eleanor glanced in the rearview
mirror. "It isn't ready yet."

"When will it be ready?"

"I'm not sure, baby."

"I'm not a baby."

"Of course not," Eleanor said. "It's just like I call you 'sweetie' sometimes."

"I am Manuel," Hattie said.

"Right," Eleanor said. "Manuel."

"Manuel isn't afraid," Hattie said to the rearview mirror, her eyes serious beneath her dark bangs.

Eleanor hadn't told her about the rats, but Hattie's faultless antennae caught every change in the wind, and she had picked up on Eleanor's anxiety, as she always did.

Eleanor wished that she, too, had an alter ego who wasn't afraid.

THE TWO SISTERS had lived apart once, for four months in 1952. Sylvia, who was older, was going to marry a man she'd met in Galveston. But she was riding in his car one evening when she felt a wash of cold fear and told him to stop and pull over.

"My sister has been in an acci-
dent," she said.

A phone call confirmed it. Lili
had fallen down the stairs and
hadn't woken up. The young man
drove Sylvia straight to the hospital, where the nurses had already
shaved Lillian's head for surgery.
The doctors were going to open her
skull, a very dangerous operation.
Sylvia stroked her sister's pretty
face. An orderly came and stood be-

hind her, ready to wheel the unconscious Lillian away.

"It's time to wake up now," Sylvia
had said. "Lili, listen. It's time to
wake up."

And Lili did. She opened her blue
eyes and gazed at Sylvia with such
sweetness. "I'm thirsty," she said in a
small voice. The orderly fetched the
doctor, who was amazed.

Lili was not the same after her fall
and couldn't remember things well.

So Sylvia broke off her engagement to look after her. The young man she'd intended to marry was sent to Korea, where he was killed, and the sisters moved in together in the two-story blue house. Sylvia began teaching school, and Lili crocheted blankets and made the curtains.

Now Sylvia peered out the window, through the gap in those curtains. A car was parked the wrong way on the street. A red car. She knew it shouldn't be parked that way.

That scruffy, pink-haired girl had left her feeling disturbed, knocking at just the wrong moment. People had tried to interfere before, but Sylvia had always stood her ground. Lili had, too, when she was able.

They'd had a dog first, who could guard the door: a loyal boxer named Hercules, who loved Lili and slept at her feet. When he died, Sylvia thought Lili might never get over it. Next they had an indifferent and yappy schnauzer, some haughty cats, a parakeet, and a series of finches that reproduced and died so quickly that it was impossible to get attached. Loving finches was like loving a box of tissues: one was plucked out, and crumpled, and gone.

And then came the new era. When Sylvia first noticed the rats' pellet droppings in the pantry, she suggested they get a trap. But Lili had cried out as if in pain.

"You can't kill them!" she said. "Listen to them! They have *plans*!"

So Sylvia listened, and she began to understand what her sister meant. The sounds in the walls were not the random scufflings of an inferior species. The rats would move an object deliberately and position it with a small thunk. Then drag something else beside it. They might have been arranging furniture in a small living room. They were intelligent beings.

Lili, at home all day, had seen them do remarkable things. They could steal a whole egg and carry it away. One rat clutched it and lay on his back, and the other dragged him by his tail. Lili had put eggs on the floor to test them, and hidden to watch. Soon they became trusting, and would just eat the egg where it was, no need to be coy.

At Lili's urging—because Lili was generous and wanted to share—Sylvia had taken their tamest pet to school, and the children had been delighted. He was an unusually sleek, handsome creature, and the

children had let him run around
their little necks. They fed him
cheese. They called him Templeton,
after the clever, greedy glutton in
Charlotte's Web. Sylvia was teaching
them reverence for all living things,
showing them that we share the
planet with other species, no better
or worse than our own.

But then the parents—the awful
parents—had marched in screaming
of disease, just like that pink-haired
girl at the door. Of *rabies*, even, of all

the ridiculous things. And that was the end of teaching for Sylvia.

She looked out through the curtains again. Was someone watching her from that red car? The glare on the windshield made it impossible to tell.

A rat moved across the mantel behind her. Sylvia never made a fire in the fireplace; it would disturb too many nests. She went to her sister's room. They had moved their beds downstairs years ago with the help of a neighbor—now dead—because it was too difficult to be always running up and down. So Lili slept in what once had been the dining room, and looked so peaceful. Her breathing was barely perceptible. Sylvia sat beside her and touched her face.

"Lili," she said. "It's time to wake up."

Lili didn't move. Beneath her sister's time-ravaged face, Sylvia saw the child's smooth one, the face she cherished.

"Lili," she said. "They're coming. Wake up."

But Lili was silent.

"Lillian," she said, lightly slapping her cheek. "They will take you away from me."

Nothing, just shallow breathing. Sylvia looked out the side window at the sycamore beyond the fence next door.

I have a small child, the pink-haired girl had said. There was a word for the way she'd said it, but

Sylvia couldn't think what it was. As if having a child gave you all the rights in the universe, and having a sister gave you nothing. As if that girl was better than other people just because she had spawned another human being. *Sanctimonious*—that was the word. Sylvia was pleased to have recovered it. She was not so far gone yet. She had produced *unfeigned* at the door—she was proud of that, too.

Dangerously infested, the girl

had said. But rats were cleaner than people. People were filthy creatures. If the health department came now, with Lili unwell, they wouldn't understand. They would claim that Sylvia couldn't take care of her sister. At the hospital they would put tubes in her sister's thin arms. Lili's body was like dry sticks beneath the bedcovers. She should be moved soon. Otherwise there would be problems, bedsores.

If Sylvia called the hospital her-

self, then they might understand
that she had the situation under con-
trol. She was a responsible person,
and they would let her have her sister back. But the telephone no lon-
ger worked. The wires were chewed
through, and Sylvia had trouble re-
membering the bills.

She could ask to use the phone
at that big, ugly new house, but the
people there had been such a bother. They had sent that young lawyer
to say they were going to sue if she

didn't get rid of the rats. She had said that no pansy was going to frighten her, and the young man had looked as surprised as if she had struck him. But he certainly was a pansy, in his tight trousers and no tie. She wasn't so old that she didn't know *that*.

Up the street was a neighbor she knew, but he was an ancient enemy. He had asked Lili to go to the movies once and Lili had wept, want-

ing to go. Sylvia had been furious.
He would have taken advantage of
the fact that she was like a child,
but how could she explain that to
Lili? It had made so much trouble,
that stupid invitation to the picture
show.

She went back to her sister's bed.
There was a scrambling noise from
the second floor. Something being
dragged. Sylvia hadn't been up there
lately. Her knees hurt too much, and,

if she was honest, she was a little afraid. The rats had *plans*, Lili had said.

"Lili," she said. "You simply *must* wake up."

ELEANOR DROPPED HATTIE off at school the next morning, in the red Manuel shirt her mother had washed. She still needed to get the green one from the new house. She wrote on her hand in blue ballpoint: GREEN SHIRT.

She would also have to check the

traps, which filled her with dread. She'd wanted to become a home-owner, an independent person, a full-fledged adult, and instead she'd become an animal trapper. Maybe she and Hattie could live in the woods, roasting varmints on sticks.

The thought made her laugh—a giddy, helpless laugh—until she saw the dead rat by the refrigerator. Its mouth was open in protest, teeth visible, neck snapped by the trap. Its fur looked soft. Eleanor shuddered.

It was strange how any loss of life caused revulsion, even if you had intended it. She turned away, fumbled with the phone, left a message for the exterminator.

In Hattie's room, she found the green T-shirt, averting her eyes from the trap in the closet, and set it on the kitchen counter with her phone, where she couldn't forget it. Then she heard a noise. At first it sounded like a siren. Next she thought it was a smoke alarm, but it was too faint.

The sound grew closer and she realized it was a human voice, and it was keening.

She crept toward the front door, and the old woman from next door stumbled into the house. Her eyes were wide with panic. She was tiny, viewed whole, without a door to shield her: a shriveled being. "Help me!" she moaned. "Help!" She grabbed Eleanor's arm with a claw-like grip.

"What happened?" Eleanor asked.

"Please!" the woman said. That evil smell of madness and neglect filled the hall.

Eleanor drew back. "I don't understand," she said.

The woman limped as she dragged Eleanor out the door and around the fence. They took the front steps slowly, the old woman bringing one foot up to meet the other, toward the peeling front door.

"Wait!" Eleanor said, with a burst of clarity. "Is she sick? Is your sister sick?"

The cloudy blue eyes turned toward her. "Yes," the old woman whispered.

"Let's call an ambulance," Eleanor said. She didn't want to go through that door. "I'll get my phone. I don't even know your name."

The woman shook her head. "Sylvia. My name is Sylvia. No ambulance. They'll take her away."

"The police, then," Eleanor said.

"No!"

"I don't think I can help you."

"Please come," Sylvia begged. She pushed open the door into the yawning, reeking darkness.

The smell made Eleanor choke, and the room was dim and cluttered. Swift, dark shapes moved along the streaked and greasy baseboards. She could hear them everywhere. In her rolled-up jeans, her ankles felt naked and exposed. She pressed her free hand over her mouth and nose. The old woman, limping, pulled her toward the back of the house.

A decaying dining table had been shoved against the wall, piled with china plates, newspapers, unopened mail, garbage. The windows were grimy and fly-spotted. One window looked out on the fence and the syca-more, beyond which was Eleanor's little house, her hope of a new life. In the middle of the room was an empty bed—or Eleanor thought at first that it was empty. It was covered with a surprisingly clean white sheet. And beneath the sheet something seemed to be struggling to breathe.

Eleanor gasped, in spite of the foul air. The sister! Why had Sylvia covered her up? She must be horribly shrunken.

Sylvia stared at the bed in horror. "Oh," she moaned.

"She's alive," Eleanor whispered.

"My sister," Sylvia said. "I wanted to protect her."

"But she needs to breathe," Eleanor said. She reached for the edge of the sheet and tugged it toward them, and then wished she hadn't.

Two fat rats sat alongside the sister's throat. The flesh was torn, the cheek half-devoured. The rats looked up when Eleanor pulled the sheet away, but they didn't run. They were used to Sylvia watching them eat; they had her blessing. The unconscious sister's chest rose, a ragged breath.

"No!" Sylvia screamed, and she lunged forward. The rats darted away, but not with the preternatural quickness of wild animals. They waited like pets to see if this was a game. "Stay away!" she cried. "Help me!"

Eleanor turned for the door. A rat ran past her bare ankle and she staggered away.

Outside in the bright day, the air burst from her lungs and she filled them with clean air. It was bracing, like cold water rushing over her. She put her hands on her knees and tried to concentrate on breathing. A crow hopped up on the curb and gave her a beady look, black feathers glinting turquoise in the sunlight.

The exterminator pulled up in his clean white truck, and Eleanor had never been so glad to see anyone. He could help. He would know who to call. He would know what to do.

WHEN THE AMBULANCE and social services finally left, Eleanor went to pick up Hattie at school, just before they would start charging her for being late. Her skin felt filmy and unclean, the oily smell in her nostrils and her pores. Now it was in her car.

"Will we go to the new house now?" Hattie asked.

"Not yet," Eleanor said. The exterminator had said that clearing the house would take days, and a lot of garbage bags. She might not want to see it.

At her parents' house, Eleanor put her clothes in the washing machine and started it. Then she stood under a hot shower for a long time. She washed her hair and scrubbed her face in the fragrant steam. Finally she got out, rubbed her hair with one of her mother's fresh towels, and put on clean clothes.

Her mother, expecting them, had overshopped. The fruit basket on the kitchen counter looked like a Dutch still life: lush abundance. Oranges and tangerines and golden pears. The sink and the counter were so clean they shone. Hattie was at the kitchen table, drawing something with circles.

Eleanor took an apple, even though she didn't want it. "So," she said, not sure if she should be addressing Hattie or Manuel. "What did you learn at school today?"

"The solar system."

"Cool." She ruffled her daughter's soft hair. She wanted to scoop her up and squeeze her, but Hattie would twist away, intent on her drawing. The circles in the picture must be planets. "What did you learn about it?"

"Jupiter is the biggest."

"Right," Eleanor said. "Which one has rats?"

Hattie looked up sharply.

"I meant *rings*!" Eleanor said, feeling her face flush. "Which one has rings?"

"Saturn," Hattie said, still watching her.

"Yes!" Eleanor said.

"Earth has rats," Hattie said.

"True."

Eleanor's mother came in and rearranged the fruit basket to fill in for the lost apple, to make it more aesthetically pleasing. Eleanor felt her chest tighten.

"How was the house?" her mother asked.

"I'll tell you later."

"Did you get the G-R-E-E-N shirt?"

"Oh, God." The ballpoint reminder on her hand was faded from the shower. "Will you watch her? I'll run back up."

"You should dry your hair first," her mother said.

"It's warm out."

"Still. It gets cold at night."

Eleanor got in the car. The streets were deserted except for the ghostly rats that seemed to be always at the corners of her vision now, scuttling away. The house was like the amulet cursed by gypsies that she had read about as a child. To save yourself, you had to look an unsuspecting young victim in the eye and put the amulet in her hand as a gift, as it had been given. The curse continued until a pure-hearted girl destroyed the amulet, refusing to pass it on.

Eleanor wondered what her broker had known, talking about manna from heaven. She was going to talk to a lawyer now, and take photographs, and find out who had known what. It wouldn't be neat like the smashing of an amulet. It would take time, but she would break the curse. When the exterminator was finished, she would disclose everything, and then she would sell her house to someone who could have a future there. In the meantime, she would try very hard to be kind to her mother.

The street was quiet when she pulled up. Adult protective services had taken Sylvia away, screaming. They would bathe her and put her in some strange institutional room, terrified and grieving, possibly restrained. The sister had been loaded into an ambulance on a stretcher, but Eleanor didn't think she would live.

Eleanor had always believed, without thinking about it, that to grow old you first had to grow up. And she had so far avoided doing that. She was still living with her parents, locked in her old teenage struggle with her mother, hoping to please and surprise her father. But the ancient sisters had plucked a deep, resonating note of fear down in her belly. There was no loophole in time, and no escape. And to grow old without growing up made it far worse. She would be old someday, unless something worse happened, but not like that. *Please*, not like that.

She let herself into the house. The green Manuel T-shirt was on the counter where she had left it, the new trap in the kitchen waiting, baited with peanut butter, sinister and unsprung. She thought of Sylvia's keening wail, and the memory was so sharp that she thought she heard it again and felt the clawing grip on her arm.

She grabbed the green shirt and locked up the house. Manuel was not afraid, and she would not give Hattie reason to be.

About the author

MAILE MELOY is the best-selling author of a middle-grade trilogy, two novels, and two story collections, including *Both Ways Is*

the Only Way I Want It, which was one of *The New York Times Book Review*'s 10 Best Books of 2009. Her stories have been published in *The New Yorker, Granta, Zoetrope*, and *The Paris Review*. She has received the Aga Khan Prize for Fiction, the PEN/Malamud Award, the Rosenthal Foundation Award from the American Academy of Arts and Letters, and a Guggenheim Fellowship. In 2007 she was chosen as one of *Granta*'s Best Young American Novelists. She lives in Los Angeles.